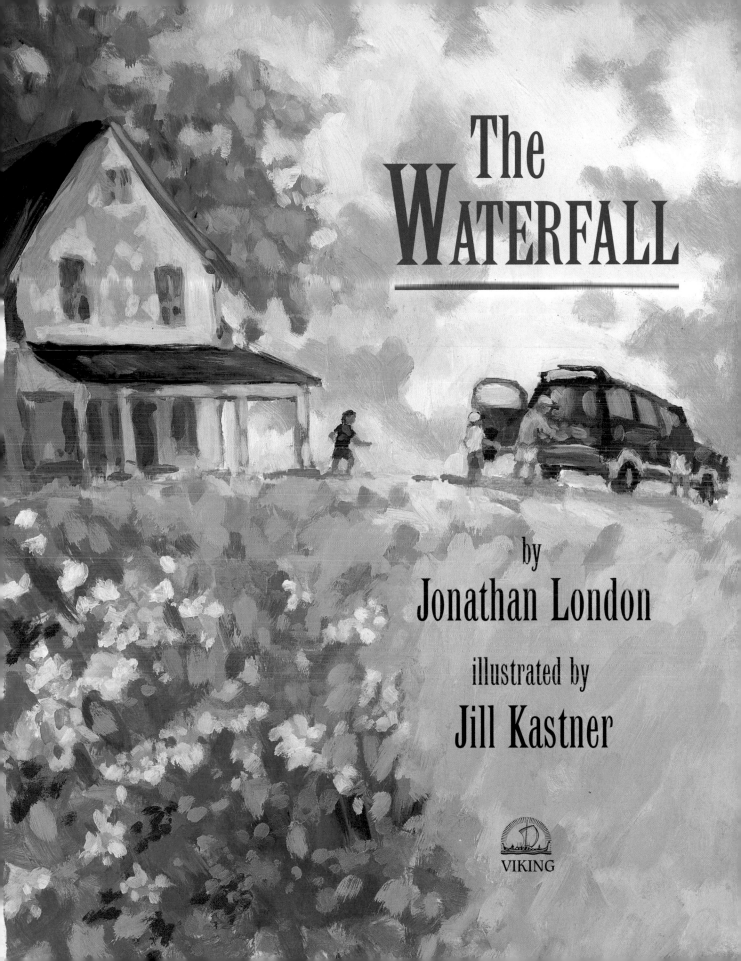

The WATERFALL

by

Jonathan London

illustrated by

Jill Kastner

VIKING

VIKING
Published by the Penguin Group
Penguin Putnam Books for Young Readers, 345 Hudson Street, New York, New York 10014, U.S.A.

Penguin Books Ltd, Registered Offices: Harmondsworth, Middlesex, England

First published in 1999 by Viking, a member of Penguin Putnam Books for Young Readers.

Text copyright © Jonathan London, 1999
Illustrations copyright © Jill Kastner, 1999

LIBRARY OF CONGRESS CATALOGING-IN-PUBLICATION DATA
London, Jonathan, date
The waterfall / by Jonathan London ; illustrated by Jill Kastner.
p.   cm.
Summary: Two brothers and their parents share a wild and wonderful backpacking trip
during which they discover a magnificent waterfall and climb to the top of it.
ISBN 0-670-87617-8
[1.Hiking—Fiction. 2. Rock climbing—Fiction.] I. Kastner, Jill, ill. II.Title.
PZ7.L8432Wat 1999 [E]—dc21 98-7828 CIP AC

Printed in Hong Kong · Set in Caxton Book
1 3 5 7 9 10 8 6 4 2

For Gene Berson and Steve Schutzman,
friends of the waterfall
—*J. L.*

To Joyce and Jim Rice
—*J. K.*

It was the middle of July
when we drove way up into the mountains
and backpacked up a creek.

The banks were lined with poison oak,
so we waded through the cold water—

hip deep for my parents,
chest deep for us—
our backpacks balanced on our heads.

We set up camp on a sandy flat
beside a pool in a ring of boulders.
What a swimming hole!
My brother and I stripped down
and skinny-dipped, diving and tumbling
in the diamond-clear water.
"Why's it called 'skinny-dipping'?" I asked.
Nobody knew

We hiked farther upstream, against little rapids,
picking our way among slippery boulders.
Suddenly we heard a roaring sound,
and as we came around a bend,
we saw what was causing it.

A huge waterfall! It rose high above us,
higher than the tallest pines.
Only a few wet ferns
clung to the steep rock slope.
A rainbow glowed in the roaring mist.
"Wow!" I said. "Let's climb it!"
"No way," said Dad. "End of the road."

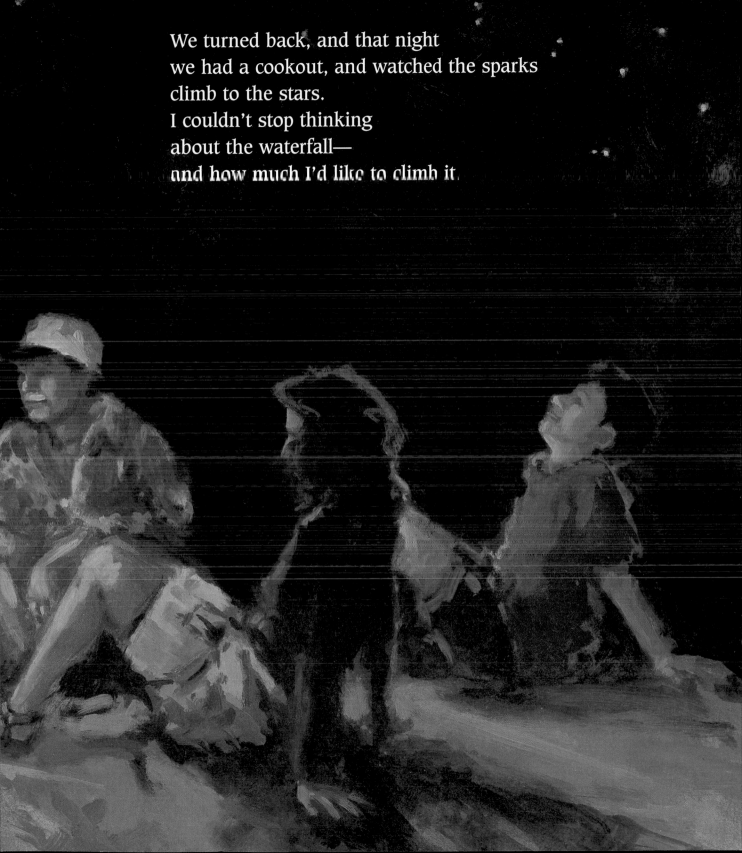

We turned back, and that night
we had a cookout, and watched the sparks
climb to the stars.
I couldn't stop thinking
about the waterfall—
and how much I'd like to climb it.

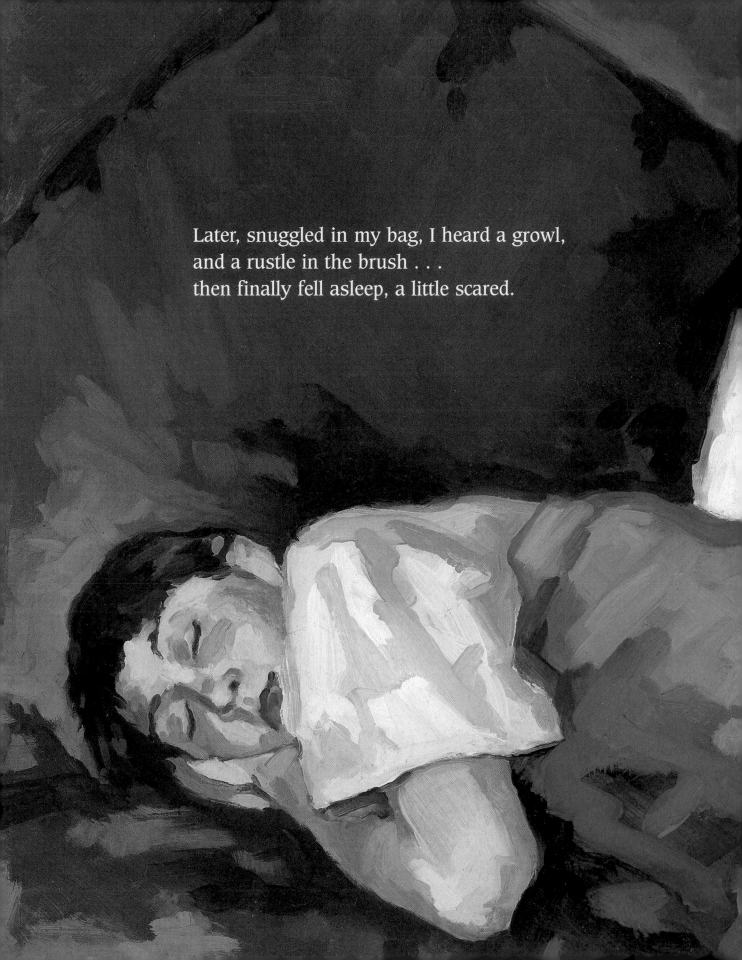

Later, snuggled in my bag, I heard a growl,
and a rustle in the brush . . .
then finally fell asleep, a little scared.

In the morning we found tracks.
"A mountain lion," said Dad.
"It must have come down for water."
It made my heart feel big and wild,
like when I saw the waterfall.
"Let's go climb the falls!" I said.
"It can't be done," said Dad,
"but let's go anyhow!"

The sun was hot as a bonfire.
We cut leaves of Indian rhubarb
as wide as elephants' ears,
and tied them on our heads with vine
to keep us cool. Then we waded
against the little rapids
deep into the canyon.
I was the first one to the waterfall.
"Let's go up," I said.
My brother grinned. "If *you* go, *I* will," he said.

I scouted a way, alongside the falls,
and then we climbed like mountain goats.
Mom hollered, "Be careful!" as if we wouldn't,
and we inched our way up and up—
the tips of our toes gripping thin ledges,
our fingers finding cracks. Sometimes
rocks pulled out, but we clung like glue.
We had to. The waterfall roared by our ears
into a great rumbling, boiling witch's cauldron
far below. "I'm scared," said my brother.
I said, "Just don't look down."

Near the top, a scrawny river willow
poked out of the rock. It was just the grip
we needed to pull ourselves up . . . up . . .

and over the edge.
When we stood at the top, we slapped five,
and shouted down, "HEY MOM, DAD!
IT'S LIKE A WHOLE OTHER WORLD UP HERE!
COME ON UP! YOU CAN DO IT!"
And I did a little dance.

Mom looked at Dad, Dad looked at Mom.
Then Mom started climbing, and Dad followed—
I couldn't believe my eyes!
I lay on my belly and shouted directions.
"No, not *that* ledge—try the one up to your right!"
I never felt more anxious—seeing my
parents clinging to that sheer rock—
or more proud, either.
Then I heard a shout and my heart jumped into my mouth.

But it was a shout of triumph!
My folks pulled themselves up, up,
and over the top.
"We *did* it!" Mom beamed, breathing hard.
"You *did* it!" I echoed. "Dad, I thought
you said it couldn't be done!"
"It *can't*," he said,
grinning like a grizzly bear.

Then all together, we continued upstream.
"Look!" I shouted.
A big piece of driftwood was wedged between boulders.
"It looks just like a dancer!"
It was river-smooth, polished by water.
It looked like a boy whirling around in joy.
"Can we take it home?" I asked.
"As a kind of souvenir?"
"If you can carry it," said Dad, "you can keep it."

It was about the hardest thing I ever did,
but I lugged that heavy driftwood back out. . . .

And now it stands in our yard.
Some people think it's a sculpture.
We just call it
"The Dancer."
Whenever I look at it,
it reminds me of the waterfall—

and makes my heart feel
big and wild.